Learning to Read, Step by Step!

Ready to Read   Preschool–Kindergarten
• big type and easy words • rhyme and rhythm • picture clues
For children who know the alphabet and are eager to
begin reading.

Reading with Help   Preschool–Grade 1
• basic vocabulary • short sentences • simple stories
For children who recognize familiar words and sound out
new words with help.

Reading on Your Own   Grades 1–3
• engaging characters • easy-to-follow plots • popular topics
For children who are ready to read on their own.

Reading Paragraphs   Grades 2–3
• challenging vocabulary • short paragraphs • exciting stories
For newly independent readers who read simple sentences
with confidence.

Ready for Chapters   Grades 2–4
• chapters • longer paragraphs • full-color art
For children who want to take the plunge into chapter books
but still like colorful pictures.

STEP INTO READING® is designed to give every child a successful
reading experience. The grade levels are only guides. Children can progress
through the steps at their own speed, developing confidence in their
reading, no matter what their grade.

Remember, a lifetime love of reading starts with a single step!

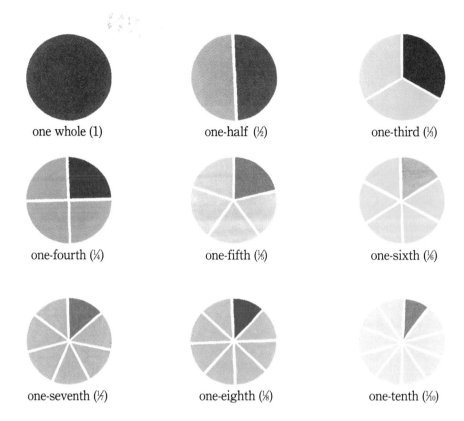

one whole (1)   one-half (½)   one-third (⅓)

one-fourth (¼)   one-fifth (⅕)   one-sixth (⅙)

one-seventh (⅐)   one-eighth (⅛)   one-tenth (⅒)

Text copyright © 2006 by Joy N. Hulme
Illustrations copyright © 2006 by Lizzy Rockwell
All rights reserved.
Published in the United States by Random House Children's Books, a division of
Random House, Inc., New York.

STEP INTO READING, RANDOM HOUSE, and the Random House colophon are registered trademarks of
Random House, Inc.

www.stepintoreading.com

Educators and librarians, for a variety of teaching tools, visit us at
www.randomhouse.com/teachers

Library of Congress Cataloging-in-Publication Data
Hulme, Joy N.
Mary Clare likes to share / by Joy N. Hulme ; illustrated by Lizzy Rockwell.
p. cm. — (Step into reading. A step 2 book, Math reader)
SUMMARY: Mary Clare divides treats into halves, thirds, or other fractional parts to make sure
that each of her friends or family members can enjoy an equal share.
ISBN-10: 0-375-83421-4 (trade)—ISBN-10: 0-375-93421-9 (lib. bdg.)
ISBN-13: 978-0-375-83421-9 (trade)—ISBN-13: 978-0-375-93421-6 (lib. bdg.)
[1. Sharing—Fiction. 2. Food—Fiction. 3. Fractions—Fiction.] I. Rockwell, Lizzy, ill. II. Title.
III. Step into reading. Step 2 book.
PZ8.3.H878Mar 2006   [E]—dc22   2005023036

Printed in the United States of America

10 9 8 7 6 5 4 3 2 1   First Edition

STEP INTO READING®

STEP 2

Mary Clare Likes to Share

A Math Reader

By Joy Hulme

Illustrated by Lizzy Rockwell

Random House 🏠 New York

Mary Clare

likes to eat.

She likes to share
each tasty treat.

"Come with me,"
she says to Lee.

They cross the yard
and climb a tree.

She picks one pear
for two to share.

One-half a pear
for each is fair.

At school today,
two classmates come
to split a muffin
with their chum.

She cuts the muffin
into three.
"One-third for you
and you and me!"

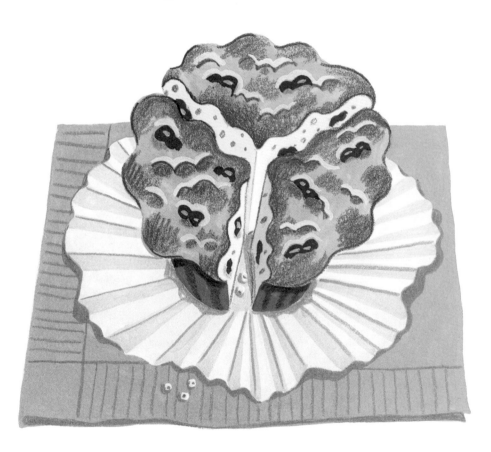

Three children knock
on Mary's door.

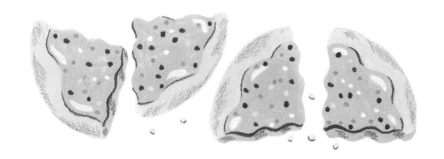

She breaks one cookie
into four.

One-fourth is right
for just one bite!

Four friends stop over
after school
for fresh-baked pie,
once it is cool.

One-fifth a pie
for each to try!

Five cousins come—
now six are there.
Each one will eat
a juicy share.

One-sixth for each
to munch with lunch.

Seven friends share
one melon slice.

One-seventh each,
as cool as ice.

"Can eight pals split
one pizza, please?"

One-eighth for each
with stretchy cheese.

Mary Clare
wants to share
her birthday
with friends everywhere!

Mary Clare calls all

to say—

"Please come and share

my special day!"

Her brother Lee
climbs down the tree.
Nate, Jill, and Kate
roll in on skates.
Gordon swings in
on the gate.

Then Cousin Mike
comes on his bike
with little Ike,
who rides a trike.

Nine kids will come,
one by one.
Ten kids in all
will share the fun!

They all bring gifts
for Mary Clare.
She is glad
her friends are there.

She baked a nice, big
birthday cake.

She cuts one piece
for each to take.

How Mary Clare
so loves to share!
"Happy birthday,
Mary Clare!"